Three Cheers for Kid McGear!

SHERRI DUSKEY RINKER AND AG FORD

chronicle books san francisco

One day at the construction yard
five friends are building, working hard.
Flatbed drives into the site. *Vroom! Vroom!*
Her secret load is strapped down tight.

The tarp comes off. And there, SURPRISE!
The crew cannot believe their eyes:
Five trucks *STOP!* and turn and stare
at the tiny truck that's sitting there.

Clean and shiny, all brand-new,
with lots of cool attachments, too!

With a scoop on her front end,
she gives a turn, a twist, a bend.

And vaults off Flatbed, in one swoop!

Beep! Beep!
"Hello!" she says, and greets the group.

“Wow! Now, who do we have here?”
“I’m a skid steer—Kid McGear!”

"I'm here to pitch in—in any way—
to help you guys get done today!

I'm here to work, to have a turn,
I want to join the team—and learn!

I'm the new kid on your crew!
So . . . is there something I can do?"

"Kid, we have a huge job here,
we have a ton of ground to clear.

I think, Kid, you are just too small,
to be much help 'round here, at all."

“I saw your trick, that’s fancy stuff!
But you don’t look quite strong enough
to jump in here and do your share . . .
maybe . . . just stay over there?”

The trucks drive off to clear the land.
"No problem, guys, I understand.
I'll help out some other day,"
Kid says, as she turns away.
The big trucks go back to working hard
clearing the construction yard.

And then . . .

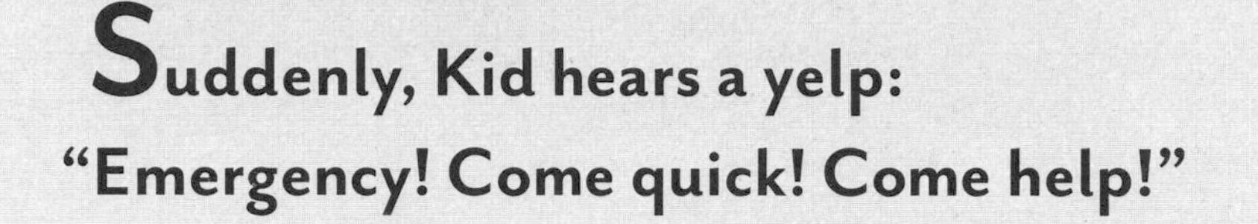

Suddenly, Kid hears a yelp:
"Emergency! Come quick! Come help!"

SCREECH! Kid stops and spins around,
revs and heads right toward the sound.

All the trucks start rolling—fast,
speeding toward the cliff, full blast.

But Kid McGear goes turbo-burst,
and, so, she gets there fast—and first!

Working on a steep hillside,
the trucks began to slip and slide.
Now, trapped in trees,
with mud and rubble,
Excavator's in big trouble!
Bulldozer is in trouble, too . . .

But Kid McGear knows what to do!
First, so that she doesn't slip,
Kid puts on tracks, so she can grip.

She stops a moment, takes a look,
and, quickly, grabs her grapple hook.
In one smooth and steady swipe,
she grabs a load of steel pipe.

Support is needed, to begin,
Kid's power driver slams them in.

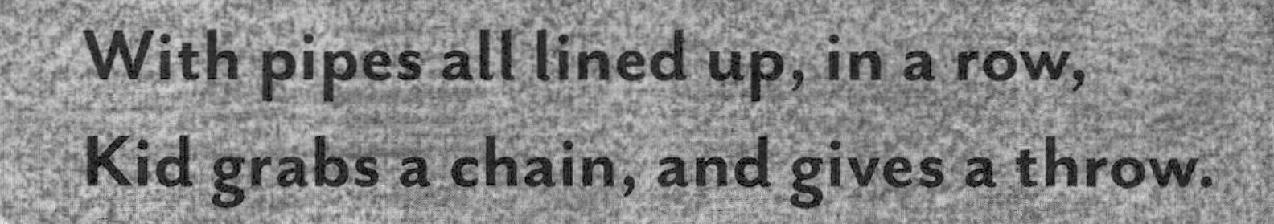

With pipes all lined up, in a row,
Kid grabs a chain, and gives a throw.

Kid rolls downhill, brave and sure,
and wraps each truck, so they're secure.

Kid's giant scissors—power shears—
cut tangled limbs. Then her blade clears.
"Now, we need something," says the Kid,
"to help make sure that they don't skid."

"Here! I'll dump this load of sand
for traction on this slippery land!"
Kid rolls into each small space,
and pushes sand right into place.

Then Kid sees a giant rock.
It has Bulldozer trapped and blocked!

And with a roar, the boulder splits.
Crane Truck clears away the rubble,
lifting each piece without trouble.

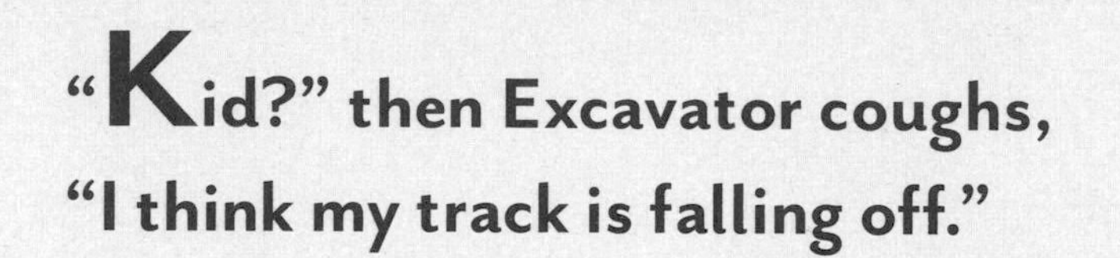

"Kid?" then Excavator coughs,
"I think my track is falling off."

Excavator shifts onto his scoop
to pull his track out from the goop.

Forklift on, lickety-split,
Kid rolls down and fixes it.

Working at full speed, nonstop,
the chain's tied to the pipes, up top.
"Cement Mixer, we need your weight!
Hit low gear, stay strong and straight!
Now, everybody, PULL!" Kid shouts.
The others rev hard, helping out.
"Down there, you guys: Start up and roll,
we'll pull and tie, to keep control!"

Soon, everyone's back on level land,
and can all get back to work, as planned.

“I’m so glad you’re all ok!”

And then Kid turns to roll away . . .

But the big trucks start to cheer
to show their thanks for Kid McGear!

They shout three times—
"Hip-hip-hooray!
Kid McGear just saved the day!"

"Please don't go, Kid.
We hope . . . you'll stay?"

Now Kid McGear has joined the crew.
Five old friends—and someone new!

SIX friends in the construction yard,
big and small, all working hard . . .

each one greater than they seem,
because they're working as a team.

For Nadalynn Rose, our own Kid McGear, and for her awesome big brothers, Jeffery and Braiden, for so warmly welcoming her to the crew.

With special thanks to Meg and Bob Lorenz, of Wm. D. Lorenz Construction, Inc., for their assistance and kindness —S.D.R.

Library of Congress Cataloging-in-Publication Data available.

ISBN 978-1-4521-5582-1

Manufactured in China.

Design by Jennifer Tolo Pierce.
Typeset in Mr. Eaves San OT.
The illustrations in this book were rendered in Neocolor wax oil crayons.

10 9 8 7 6 5 4 3

Chronicle Books LLC
680 Second Street
San Francisco, California 94107

Chronicle Books—we see things differently. Become part of our community at www.chroniclekids.com.